IDIOMATIX

COW PA

The cow that keeps putting her hoof in it!

GW00731416

In fields far far away is Mucky Feet Farm. It is home to farmers, Fran and Stan, and farmyard animals like Cow Pat who live in the haybale barn.

Cow Pat is black and white with long legs, large hooves and a big brass bell around her neck. The other animals adore Cow Pat, but she has the unfortunate habit of putting her hoof in it!

"Are you looking forward to your party, Dog Paula?" asks Cow Pat.

"My party?" replies Dog Paula.

"Yes, your party!" confirms Cow Pat, "Your surprise party!"

"You mean the party…" responds Dog Paula, barking, "…I'm not to know about!"
"Oops! Sorry, Dog Paula," apologises Cow Pat, "I've put my hoof in it!"

"I'm so excited about the party, Cat Kitty?" says Cow Pat.

"What party?" asks Cat Kitty.

"Dog Paula's surprise party!" replies Cow Pat.

"You mean the surprise party…" responds Cat Kitty, meowing, "…to which I'm not invited!"

"Oops! Sorry, Cat Kitty," apologises Cow Pat, "I've put my hoof in it!"

"What do you think of the party, Duck Ling Su?" asks Cow Pat.

"I think it's a success!" replies Duck Ling Su.

"I think it's boring!" declares Cow Pat.

"This is the party…" responds Duck Ling Su, quacking, "…I organised for Dog Paula!"
"Oops! Sorry, Duck Ling Su," apologises Cow Pat, "I've put my hoof in it!"

"This is a lovely cup of tea, Chicken Cooper," remarks Cow Pat.
"Yes, it is!" replies Chicken Cooper, "Earl Grey's finest!
"But who made the sandwiches?" asks Cow Pat, "They taste foul!"

"The sandwiches..." responds Chicken Cooper, clucking, "...are made by me!"
"Oops! Sorry, Chicken Cooper," apologises Cow Pat, "I've put my hoof in it!"

"Who's that pig in the corner, Pig Penry?" asks Cow Pat.

"Which pig?" replies Pig Penry, "There are many."

"That big fat pig!" points Cow Pat.

"That big fat pig…" responds Pig Penry, snorting, "…is my sister!"

"Oops! Sorry, Pig Penry," apologises Cow Pat, "I've put my hoof in it!"

"I saw someone who looks like you, Goose Chasey," begins Cow Pat.

"Who's that?" replies Goose Chasey.

"I think she's your daughter!" informs Cow Pat, "She looks much younger than you!"

"I think you'll find…" responds Goose Chasey, quacking, "…that she is my mother!"

"Oops! Sorry, Goose Chasey," apologises Cow Pat, "I've put my hoof in it!"

"You look great, Horse Shula!" compliments Cow Pat, "I love your new haircut!"
"What do you mean?" replies Horse Shula.
"The ponytail with the bow-tied ribbons really suits you!" says Cow Pat.

"I've had a ponytail with ribbons..." responds Horse Shula, neighing, "...ever since I've known you!"

"Oops! Sorry, Horse Shula," apologises Cow Pat, "I've put my hoof in it!"

"I've just seen a sheep wearing the most dreadful woollen dress, Sheep Eugenie," says Cow Pat.

"Is it that green dress with the yellow dots?" asks Sheep Eugenie.

"Yes, that's the one!" replies Cow Pat, "Isn't it disgusting?"

"That green dress…" responds Sheep Eugenie, bleating, "…is a dress I knitted!
"Oops! Sorry, Sheep Eugenie," apologises Cow Pat, "I've put my hoof in it!"

"I've put my hoof in it with the other sheep!" relays Cow Pat to Goat Herod, "They're ignoring me."

"What do you mean *the other sheep?*" asks Goat Herod.

"The other sheep like you!" replies Cow Pat.

"I'm not a sheep…" responds Goat Herod, stamping, "…I'm a goat!"
"Oops! Sorry, Goat Herod," apologises Cow Pat, "I've put my hoof in it!"

"I hear you've upset everyone, Cow Pat!" says Fox Denise.

"I didn't mean to," replies Cow Pat, "but I keep putting my hoof in it!"

"I need you to put your hoof in it now?" instructs Fox Denise.

"I'm not falling for that, Fox Denise!" says Cow Pat. "I'm saying nothing!"
"No, Cow Pat," responds Fox Denise, "I need you to put your hoof in the hoof bath!"
"Oops! Sorry, Fox Denise," apologises Cow Pat. "There, I've put my hoof in it!"

**NOW LOOK OUT
FOR THE NEXT IDIOMATIX**

LAMB STEW